Welcome to the Medal Club!

@medalclubkids

First Printing, 2019

Medal Addict Press
Brooklyn, NY 11236

www.MedalClubKids.com

Dedicated to the late Stanley Manning, and future Medal Addicts.

There was only one thing Zoe hated about school, Field Day. Every year th[e] students at Stanley Academy competed in everything from the sit-up contest to the race around the track. Zoe and her best friend, Kenny, usually watched from the stands as their classmates won medal after medal. But this year, every student had to participate.

On the playground during recess, Zoe and Kenny listened to all of their friends buzz about field day.

No one was more excited than The Medal Clique.

If there was a prize to win, they won it. Only winners were allowed in The Medal Clique.

"Look, Kat is already getting her group ready."

Kenny noticed Kat, the leader of The Medal Clique, standing in the middle of the playground shouting encouragement to her friends.

here was also Bobby, the strongest kid in the fourth grade, practicing
s grip on the monkey bars. Anna, who loved to do backflips all over the
hoolyard, was practicing her landing on the net. Then there was Rico,
acticing his running so he could be the fastest kid in the fourth grade.

Ve already know The Medal Clique are going to win everything,"
ghed Zoe.

et's try to have fun anyway." Kenny said trying to make Zoe feel better.

Field Day was going exactly as Zoe expected. Kat earned a medal for the most pull-ups. Rico earned a medal for climbing up the rope the fastest. Anna earned a medal and broke her cartwheel contest record. Bobby pulled five kids across the tug-of-war line, earning himself a medal, too.

Now it was time for the sprint around the track. Zoe was surprised when Kenny signed up. When the horn blew, Kenny took off running as fast as he could. He was the first person to cross the finish line.

Zoe couldn't believe it.

"Welcome to The Medal Clique," screamed Kat while the rest of the group cheered.

The next day, instead of hanging out with Zoe during recess, Kenny hung out at the jungle gym with The Medal Clique.

They gave him high fives, as he retold the story of coming in first place during the sprint.

The jungle gym was their territory and their training ground.

"You should train with us," said Bobby.

"Train for what?" asked Kenny

"The Mud is Fun Kids Obstacle Course Race is coming. You should join us," said Rico.

"Yeah, field day was just practice," chuckled Anna.

"We do it every year. We get to climb walls and crawl in mud. Then on Monday, we show up to school with medals that make Field Day medals look like toys," boasted Kat.

Kenny decided to sign up. It was official. Kenny was now a part of The Medal Clique.

Zoe was determined not to lose her best friend. She begged her parents to sign her up for the race. For the next few weeks, Zoe trained in secret. She tried to do everything The Medal Clique did on the playground.

She ran around in circles.
She tried to do push-ups.
She even jumped rope.

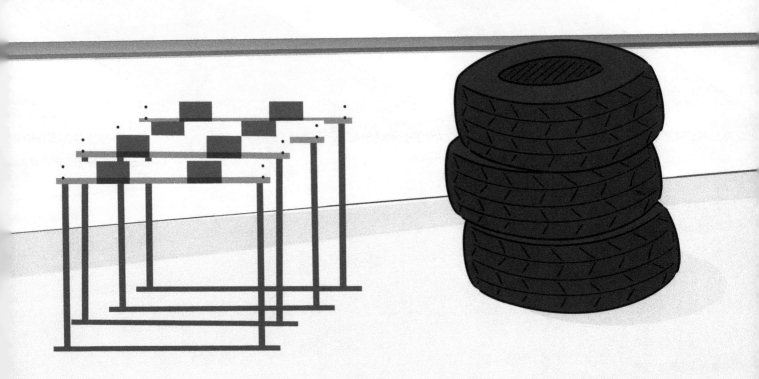

She was going to beat
The Medal Clique,
and then she and Kenny
would start their own group.

"Welcome to the 3rd Annual Mud is Fun Kids Obstacle Course Race." Announced Emcee Justin. His voice boomed over the speakers as Zoe stretched at the start line.

Kenny and
The Medal Clique spotted Zoe.
Kenny couldn't believe it. His new friends laughed.

"Today, you will get dirty. You will have fun, and you will make friends. That is the true prize!"

"She won't make it past the first obstacle," snickered Anna.
"Are you ready? Say Mud is Fun!" Emcee Justin called out.
"Mud is fun!" Shouted the kids at the start line.
"One, Two, Three, GO!" Emcee Justin blew the horn, and all of the kids ran towards the first obstacle.

From the beginning, Kenny and The Medal Clique were already ahead of everyone else. Zoe struggled to make it past the firs obstacle but was determined to catch up.

Up next was the tire flip. Bobby flipped the tire quickly.

Zoe surprised herself and flipped the tire on the first try.
She started to run to the next obstacle but noticed Anna was
having a hard time flipping her tire. Zoe ran back to help her.

Zoe and Anna then ran together towards the monkey bars. Of course, Kat zipped across, followed by the rest of The Medal Clique, yet Kenny was having a ha time. Zoe and Anna promised to stay at the obstacle until he finished.

"Don't worry. We'll catch you if you fall," Zoe assured Kenny. Kenny completed the monkey bars and joined Anna and Zoe as they ran toward the next obstacle, the rope climb.

They find Rico stuck at the rope.
"I'm afraid to climb down," said Rico.
"You got this," Zoe encouraged.
"Yea, you can do it," Kenny chimed in.
"We're here for you," screamed Anna.

They all loudly clapped and cheered
until Rico made it safely to the ground.

Zoe, Anna, Kenny, and Rico high five each other and run together to the next challenge.

Next, they arrive at the mud pit. Everyone jumped in on one end and began to climb out of the other, but they notice Bobby is stuck.

"I lost my shoe," sighs Bobby.
"C'mon everyone, let's look for Bobby's shoe!" says Zoe.
They find Bobby's shoe and run together towards the final obstacle.

On the last obstacle, Kat was tired and was struggling to pull herself up the wall.

"One more step," screamed Bobby.

"You're almost there," Kenny and Rico join in.

Kat makes it up and over the wall, followed by Bobby, Kenny, Rico, Anna, and Zoe.

They could see the finish line and started to run as fast as they could. Running was always the hardest activity for Zoe, and she stopped to take a break. The group continued to run until Kenny noticed that Zoe was not with them.

"We can't leave Zoe!" he shouted to get the attention of the group.

"C'mon man! We're at the finish line. We are about to be the top finishers again," sighs Rico.

"Did Zoe leave you at the rope climb?" asked Anna.

"Right, she helped all of us today," said Bobby.

"Remember what Emcee Justin said today?

Your friends are the biggest prize," adds Kat.

Rico nods and begins to run back toward Zoe as the rest of the group follows.

They all crossed the finish line, **together.**

Mondays at Stanley Academy was not like other schools. It was Medal Monday. Usually, The Medal Clique came to school ready to show off the medals and awards they won at their competitions and contests over the weekend. This time Zoe and Kenny joined them.

For the first time, Zoe got to hang out with The Medal Clique at the jungle gym. She was the last student the other kids thought would get to join the Clique. Another friend of theirs approached them to see if he could play.

"What are you doing here, Tim?" Rico asked.

"Medal Clique only!" Bobby added.

"You know the rules," Kat grumbled.

"C'mon everyone. Didn't we learn anything this weekend? We're all friends, right?" Zoe reminded the group.

"But we're The Medal Clique," whined Anna.

"Zoe's right, maybe we shouldn't be a clique anymore." Kenny stood up to the group.

"Alright! Medal Club on three..."

Kat started the chant.

About the Authors

Justin T. Manning and Simone Waugh are the Co-Founders of Medal Addict, Inc. Together, they have created a community that shines a spotlight on athletes of all levels, who are achieving on and off the racecourse.

About the Illustrator

Elijah Rutland is an illustrator, sneaker artist, and designer from Macon, GA. He is the creator of the Rolf meme and is most well-known for his work under the name "Fix My Sole," which he has been operating since 2015. Elijah is also currently studying graphic design at Florida A&M University.